Memoirs of a

GOLDFISH

Sleeping Bear Press

Devin Scillian and Illustrated by Tim Bowers

Sleeping Bear Press™

315 East Eisenhower Parkway, Suite 200
Ann Arbor, MI 48108
www.sleepingbearpress.com

© 2010 Sleeping Bear Press is an imprint of Gale, a part of Cengage Learning.

10 9 8

Library of Congress Cataloging-in-Publication Data

Scillian, Devin.
Memoirs of a goldfish / written by Devin Scillian ; illustrated by Tim Bowers.
p. cm.
Summary: A goldfish gives a personal account of his experiences while swimming around his bowl as it slowly fills
with fish and other accessories, only to realize when he is relocated for a cleaning how much he misses them.
ISBN 978-1-58536-507-4
[1. Goldfish—Fiction. 2. Friendship—Fiction.] I. Bowers, Tim, ill. II. Title.
PZ7.S41269Me 2010
[E]—dc22
2009037413

Printed by China Translation & Printing Services Limited,
Guangdong Province, China. 8th printing. 12/2011

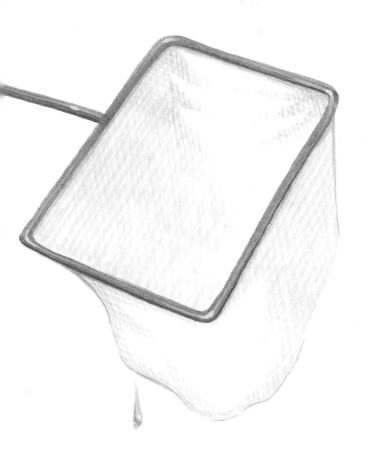

To my beautiful guppies,
Griffin, Quinn, Madison, and Christian,
who gave me the idea for this story
—D.S.

To my good friend, Stuart Thomas
—T.B.

Day One

I swam around my bowl.

Day Two

I swam around my bowl. Twice.

Day Three

I swam around my bowl.
I thought about taking a nap.
But fish don't sleep.
So I swam around my bowl.

Day Four

I got some company today.

I don't like the looks of him one bit.

He doesn't say anything. He just bubbles.

Day Five

Mr. Bubbles still hasn't said a word.
He just looks at me. I said "Hello" today.
And he said, "Ggggllllggggllll."
He's creepy.

Day Six

Today my bowl looks like a garden.
There are a bunch of plants in here now.
I guess I'll have to water them.

Great.

Day Seven

Mr. Bubbles and I now have company. He's a snail. He says his name is Mervin and he likes to eat the slime off the inside of the bowl.
He's disgusting.

Day Eight

Things are getting very crowded. While watering the plants,
I met a crab named Fred. I offered him my fin and he nearly cut it off.
Even Mr. Bubbles is afraid of him. Fred says I should stay on my side
of the bowl. "Look," I said, "the whole bowl is my side of the bowl."
He snapped his claw and Mervin fainted.

I gotta get out of here.

Day Nine

That does it. My bowl now contains a sunken pirate ship, two guppies named Rhoda and Clark, and an angelfish named Cha-Cha who says she's from Hollywood. I can't turn around without bumping into something.

At least Mervin is happy. There's more gunk on the side of the bowl every day.

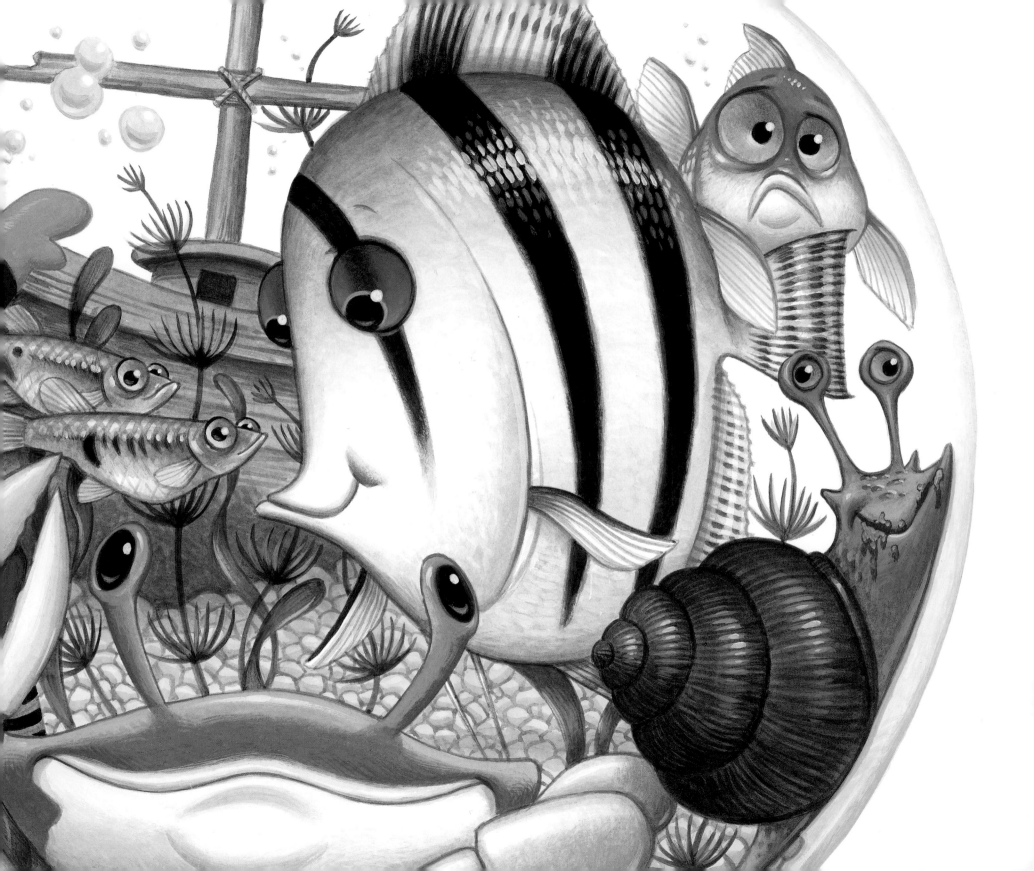

Day Ten

This is ridiculous.

I was trying to find room for a swim today when Rhoda and Clark told me they're going to have babies soon.

Like there's room for THAT.

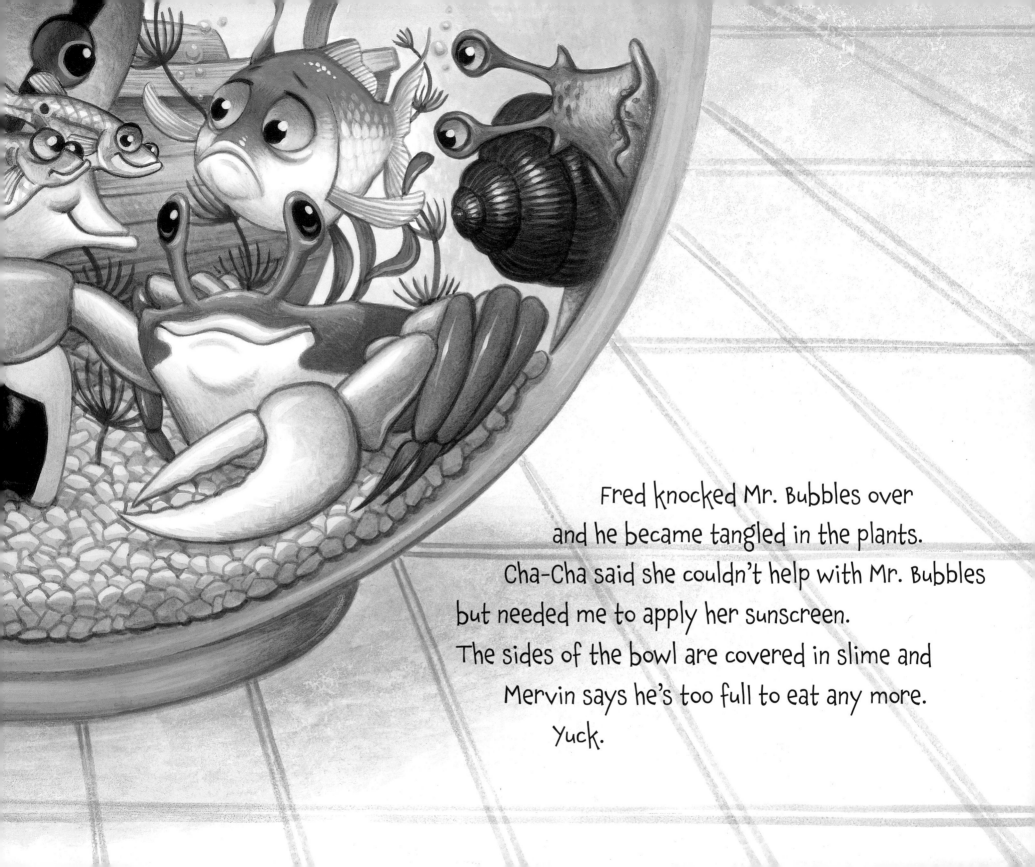

Fred knocked Mr. Bubbles over
and he became tangled in the plants.
Cha-Cha said she couldn't help with Mr. Bubbles
but needed me to apply her sunscreen.
The sides of the bowl are covered in slime and
Mervin says he's too full to eat any more.
Yuck.

Day Eleven

I'm a nervous wreck. Trying to avoid Fred, I turned
around quickly this morning and came face to face with my
reflection in a mirror. I nearly jumped out of my gills.
I don't even look like myself anymore. I need to relax.

Day Twelve

I've had it. Rhoda and Clark were racing around the bowl, Fred was fighting with Mr. Bubbles, Mervin kept belching, and Cha-Cha told me I was standing in her light.

I just lost it.

**"This is my bowl!" I screamed.
"I want my bowl back!"**

Day Thirteen

Today I got my wish. Sort of. With a whoosh, and a splash, and a clank, and a plunge, I was suddenly in a very tiny bowl of clear, pure water. Ahhh. It was small, but it was all mine. It was heavenly. I swam around my new bowl.

Twice.

But I started to wonder. What had happened to everyone?

When I last saw Mr. Bubbles, he was tangled in green. Who would help him?

Poor Mervin was probably sick as a dogfish. He needs me.

Cha-Cha will get a sunburn without me around.

What about Rhoda and Clark? Did Rhoda have her baby guppies?

There are probably a thousand of them!

They need me to make guppy bottles and change guppy diapers.

Even Fred needs me. I'm the only one who can really talk to the crabby guy.

Have they even noticed I'm gone? Does anyone miss me?

I started to cry. And that's not easy for a fish to do.

Day Fourteen

After a long, sad night there was a whoosh, and a splash, and a clank, and a plunge, and I was suddenly sprayed in the face by bubbles.

Mr. Bubbles gurgled a happy tune. Rhoda and Clark raced by me like two speedboats, followed by twelve of the cutest baby guppies you've ever seen. Mervin waved his tail at me from the nice clean glass of our enormous tank. Cha-Cha sat happily beneath an umbrella.

I think even Fred missed me.

We were all back together, and I looked around and realized I was part of a big family. I guess I must have smiled because Clark said, "You look happy."

I wanted to see for myself.
"Where's the mirror?" I asked.

"What mirror?" asked Clark.

"We don't have a mirror," said Fred.

No mirror? No wonder I didn't
look like myself.

It wasn't me I was seeing...

Her name is Gracie, and she's the color of a fresh tangerine. She's a Pisces just like me. And today we're going to swim around the tank together.

Twice.